# Puppy Tales
# The Adventures of Adam
# the Australian Shepherd

*Written by Kelly Carper Polden*

*Illustrations by Cheryl Eckenrode*

Content rights ©2007, Kelly Carper Polden.
Kelly Carper Communications, Johnson City, Texas.

ISBN 978-1-4196-7458-7

*For Adam, who inspired me
to write his story,
and for Howard,
who encouraged me to
write my first book.*

## Introducing Adam, the Australian Shepherd

My name is Adam. This is my
story. I am an Aussie, an
Australian shepherd puppy. I
like to run, jump, and play
like most dogs. I also
instinctively herd farm
animals and protect their
babies. When I herd animals,
I round them up and move them
from one place to another in the
pasture. I also protect them by keeping watch over them
and making sure other animals do not hurt them. No
one taught me to do these things. I just know how to do
them. Aussies are known for having a strong need to
guard and protect animals that are left in our care.

I am described as a tricolor Aussie. My furry coat is
copper- and cinnamon-colored, with patches of white on
my legs, belly, neck, and head. I have a patch of copper-
colored fur over one eye, which makes me look like I
have half of a mask on my face. I have bright, amber-

colored eyes that make me look intense and alert. My ears are copper-colored, too. They perk up when I hear the slightest noise. My fur is usually fairly long like my dog cousin, the Border collie. My fur gets clipped short because I live on a ranch and get covered in burrs and other prickly things when my coat is too shaggy. Before I moved to the ranch, I didn't know what a burr was. I soon found out that it is the seed of a plant that grows wild out in the country. Burrs are prickly and stick to my fur and my paws. Burrs don't hurt; they just make me look messy. But sometimes I would step on a different type of burr that has spines. Those burrs are called *goat heads* because the prickly spines are like the horns of a goat. Goat head burrs are painful when they get in my paws. I had to learn how to carefully pull them off my paw with my teeth. If I can't get a goat head burr off of me, my momma helps me by gently pulling it off my paw or carefully picking it out of my fur.

My momma is not my doggie momma, she is my human momma. I love my momma! She and my human poppa adopted me and take good care of me. They know that if I am treated right and feel loved, I love back with all my heart. They also understand that as an Aussie, I need to work, run, and play every day. Momma and Poppa taught me how to be a trail runner. We go to a nearby state park and run on the hiking trails. I can run almost ten miles now, and I am not even two years old yet! I love running. I also love living on the ranch. I have a lot of open space where I can run and play. My momma plays with me a lot. Every time we walk in the pasture to check on the horses, Momma looks for a stick to throw so that I can fetch it. Aussie's are very agile. That means we are able to move quickly and easily. I can leap into the air, catch the stick, drop to the ground, spin around in circles, and race back to Momma in just a few seconds. She always laughs and rubs my head, telling me I am a good boy. I proudly carry my stick and race around the pasture to show my toy to the horses. It is a lot of fun!

I enjoy adventures, especially the ones that I have on the ranch. I have so many stories to tell you. Momma calls my stories *puppy tales*. I hope you enjoy reading about my adventures as much as I like telling you about them.

# *Chapter 1*

## Adam Needs a Good Home

Before I met my momma and moved to the ranch, I was scared to act like a puppy. My first owner was a young woman who picked me out from a litter of pups when I was just eight weeks old. She came to my house for a visit one summer day and saw me playing on the floor with two of my puppy brothers. The woman picked me up and said I was a cute little ball of fur. It was fun when she played with me. I rolled on the floor and begged for rubs. She seemed nice, and I was ready for the adventure of a new home, even though I was still just a little pup.

That very day, my new owner took me home and named me Jake. At first, I missed my doggie momma. I also missed playing with my puppy brothers, but I thought I was going to have a nice life at my new home. I found out the hard way that my new owner didn't know how to properly care for a puppy, and I couldn't make her understand. Australian shepherds are full of energy. We were bred to work long hours on a farm or ranch. If Aussies don't work, we need to play and get good exercise every day. But my new owner was too busy to take care of me. Each day, she went to work early in the morning. In the afternoon she went to school at the nearby college. Every day, instead of being taken for a run or even for a long walk, I was kept in the bedroom of a small apartment that was part of a big building. I could hear loud voices and other sounds, but I couldn't see what was making the noise. Sometimes I would get scared because I was left alone for hours and hours each day. Australian shepherds are known to be loyal friends and companions. We want to be with our owners as much as possible to show them our affection and to protect them. My owner was rarely home with me.

Aussies are not content to lay on the floor and be *couch potatoes*. I needed to be outside so that I could run and play, but I was all by myself in the apartment. I was bored. Aussies are smart dogs. If our owners aren't around to provide guidance and discipline, we find our own way of getting exercise. But that can lead to trouble. I made a racetrack around the room to entertain myself. I would leap over furniture and knock over whatever was in my way. I had a lot of fun making up racing games. I would also chew on things, such as furniture, shoes, and clothes, because puppies need chew toys and all I had were items that I could find in my owner's room. I made a big mess that included using the room as my bathroom. I didn't mean to make that kind of mess, but I had to do it. I just couldn't hold it for hours and hours. I was really sorry. I would sit in the corner and then lie down and put my paws over my nose. I knew I would get in trouble. When my owner came home, she would get mad at me for the mess that I made during the day. I didn't like it when my owner yelled at me. It made me very sad and scared. But the next day, when I was left home alone again for hours and hours, I would do the same things because I had no choice. As I grew bigger and became older, I had even more energy. My owner didn't understand that I was just a puppy.

My owner didn't understand that I just needed to run and play. She shouldn't have left me alone for so many hours without something useful to do. This went on for a long time.

When I was almost five months old, my owner came home and became very angry with me for making a big mess in my room. She yelled at me in a very loud voice. Then she spanked me. I was so sorry and so scared. My owner grabbed me and carried me downstairs and through the apartment building. She put me in the backseat of her car. After a few minutes, she stopped yelling at me. When she was quiet for a while, I thought everything would be okay. I thought maybe we were finally going to go for a walk at the park, like we did the first week my owner took me home. Instead, she took me to the pound. We went into a small room. She shook her finger at me and said I was a very bad dog. Then she walked out of the room, slammed the door shut, and she left.

I was alone. I was sitting in the middle of a small room. I could hear loud voices coming from the other side of the door and a lot of dogs barking in the back room. I suddenly felt very lonely. I slid down to the floor and put my paws over my nose. A few minutes later, a nice lady came into the room.

She patted my head and checked me over carefully. Then she took my leash and walked me down a long hallway that was lined with metal pens. Each pen housed one or two barking dogs. Just before we reached the end of the hallway, the woman put me in a small pen. There were loud dogs all around me. I was scared. I lay down and put my paws over my nose again. I wanted to say I was sorry, but my owner never came back to see me or to take me home.

For several days, I was fed, cleaned, and played with once in a while at the pound, which I later found out was called the Humane Society. I was treated nicely by a lot of different people, but I was still scared. One week after I arrived at the Humane Society, a friendly woman came to visit me. She said that since I am a purebred Australian shepherd, I was going to be taken care of by a special group called Austin Aussie Rescue.

The nice lady took my leash and walked me to her car. I jumped into the back seat. We went for a short drive to see the *vet*, a special doctor for puppies. I

received a medical checkup and was taken to a
foster home where a nice woman took care of me.

A foster home is where abandoned puppies can get
the care and attention we need until a new owner
comes to adopt us. I was still scared. I hoped that I
would be happy at my new, short-term home.
At my foster home, a nice woman took care of me.
She wanted to help me forget about my life with my
first owner, so she renamed me Adam. I liked my
new name! I had my own puppy crate with an old
towel for my bed. I like my crate because it is a safe
place where I can sleep peacefully.

Sometimes I go into my crate when I need quiet time in my own space. It is like having my own bedroom. I try to keep it clean and neat. My foster mother let me eat inside my crate so that I didn't have to share my food with the other dogs.

My foster mother had many other dogs that I could play with every day. We lived out in the country, where we could run and play in a big fenced-in yard. The dogs became my friends, but sometimes they let me know that I was not really part of the family.

Like most animals, dogs have a chain of command, with a chief dog that is the leader and other top dogs that make the rest of us follow the chief dog's orders. I was the last dog in the pecking order, but I was part of the pack. That made me happy.

One thing that I didn't like about my foster home was the cat. I had never met a cat before, but this one made me think that I never want to meet a cat again. Each time I walked into the living room, the cat would walk over to me and act like she wanted to play. When I walked over to sniff her, she would hiss and lash out at me with her sharp claws. I quickly learned not to trust the cat. When I came into the room, I would walk around the cat in a wide circle so that she couldn't scratch me.

By early spring, I had lived at my foster home for almost three months. I was getting used to my foster home and my dog friends, but my foster mother told me that some day I would have a new owner and go to a new home. Every night, I would lie down in my crate and think about what might happen. I would get scared that my new owner would be like the first woman who took me to her home. Those thoughts would make me lay my head on the floor and cover my nose with my paws. I had to believe my foster mother when she told me that she would make sure my new owner would love me and take good care of me forever.

# *Chapter 2*
## Adam Moves to the Ranch

In late March, almost four months after I moved to my foster home, I was outside playing with my dog friends, when my foster mother called us all into the house. She told me that some people were coming to visit and they might want to adopt me. My foster mother said she would make sure they were dog-loving people who would be good to me and understand my needs. She wanted my dog friends to be inside, too, to see how the visitors would greet and treat each of us.

I ran into my crate when I heard the knock on the door. I didn't know what to do. I didn't know if I wanted to meet these people. A man and a woman walked into the room. They looked nice. They patted the heads of each of my dog friends. I crept out of my crate as my foster mother told the man and woman about me. I stayed in the corner of the room, watching everything that was happening. I liked it when the woman sat on the floor in the middle of the room and smiled at me. It made me want to meet her. I walked over to sniff her hand. She waited until I had time to decide that I liked her smell, and then she gave me a pat on the head and smiled.

I walked away to think about what I wanted to do next. I liked the way she pet me. I wondered if the man would be nice too. He let me sniff his hand and his feet as he sat in a chair, and then he smiled and rubbed my head. That was a good sign!

I walked around the room again before sitting on the floor next to the woman. As the woman talked to my foster mother, she started to nicely pat my head and stroke my back. Before I knew it, I was laying on her lap, asking her to rub my belly. She did, and it felt so nice! The man and woman spent more than an hour at my foster home. I liked the sounds of their voices. They seemed nice, and both of them were very gentle when they rubbed my head. When it was time for them to leave, the man asked me if I wanted to come and live with them. Oh yes! I ran over, sat down in front of him, and gave him my paw to shake on the deal. My foster mother laughed and said that was it; they were the best family for me.

My new family was just about to move to a home out in the country. I stayed at my foster home until they were finished moving into the new house. In early May, when it was time for me to go to my new home, my foster mother put me in the back seat of the car. She wanted to see my new home for herself, so that she could make sure it was puppy-proof, because she wanted to be sure that there wasn't anything around that could get me into trouble. As I rode in the car, I started to have second thoughts. What if that visit was all a dream? What if I didn't like my new home? What if it was like my first home? I lay down and put my head on the seat and covered my nose with my paws. I was getting scared.

My foster mother turned off the country road and drove up a long gravel driveway toward a one-story, white, stone house. The big, front pasture was wide open and filled with grass and wildflowers. Near the house was a small pasture that was surrounded by a high white fence. I stood up on the seat to get a better look. This place had a lot of room where I could run and play. My ears perked up. I thought about how much fun I could have here. As my foster mother drove onto the paved circle driveway, I could see a large white and green barn, a detached garage, a large front yard, and an even bigger back pasture. I could see three horses looking at me. They ran over to the fence to get a better look at us. Two of the horses were reddish-brown with streaks of white running down their faces. The other horse was much smaller and looked a lot like me, with copper and cinnamon patches of color all over its white body. That horse was really cute! I started to do a little dance on the back seat as I rushed from window to window to look at everything on the ranch. I was excited that this would be my new home.

As my foster mother put me on my leash and walked toward the door of the house, I could see the man and woman who had visited me. They came outside to greet us. I started to prance as I thought about how nicely they treated me. Once inside the house, though, I got a little scared again because I wasn't familiar with the inside of the house. I didn't smell the scent of dogs like I did at my foster home. I suddenly missed my dog friends. I stood close to my foster mother and was ready to turn and run at any moment. I recognized the scent of the man and woman, but I was still afraid. As soon as the woman saw me, she sat on the floor and smiled at me as she called my name. Okay, I thought, I'll let her pet me again. That was all I needed. In a few minutes I was in the woman's lap, getting my belly rubbed. It felt as good as I remembered!

The man showed me my new crate. It was just as big as the one I had at my foster home, but this one had a blue pad on the floor. I ran inside to sniff it. The pad felt soft on my paws. I did a little dance inside the crate to let everyone know that I really liked it. Then I raced out of the crate to inspect the rest of the house.

As my foster mother sat at the table and talked with the man and woman, I stood in the middle of the room, looking around at my new home. Suddenly, a cat walked into the room. *Oh no*, I thought, *not a cat!* The cat looked at me and arched its back. *Here it comes*, I thought, *that cat is going to be mean to me.* I looked around the room to see how I could walk in a wide circle, like I did at my foster home, so the cat wouldn't hiss and claw at me. But this cat didn't hiss. She started walking toward me, but she didn't have her claws out. I sat down, not sure what to do. The cat walked right up to me and rubbed her head on my front leg. She started to purr as she walked around me, nuzzling up to my back. *This looks like a cat*, I thought, *but it can't be one.* She didn't act like one. This cat seemed to be welcoming me to my new home. I carefully put my nose down close to her face and sniffed. She smelled like a cat. She kept purring and nuzzling me. I liked it! The next thing I knew I was playing … with a cat!

After about an hour, my foster mother walked over to me and gave me a big hug. She started to cry. She told me I was a good boy and that I had a nice, new home with people who would take good care of me. Then she hugged the man and woman and walked out the door.

I ran to window as she got into her car and drove away. I started to feel scared again. What if I didn't like it here? But my new owners came over and rubbed my head. They told me how glad they were to have such a good puppy. The cat came over and started to purr again as she rubbed up against my legs. I did a little dance of excitement as I ran into my new crate and looked at my new family. This was a dream come true!

# *Chapter 3*
## Adam Almost Runs Away

I almost ran away the day after I arrived at my new home. I didn't plan to run away. I had a good first night in my new home. But the next morning, my momma got in her car and drove away. I stayed home with my poppa, and I was exploring the big, fenced-in backyard, when a stranger arrived. He was wearing a bandana on his head and had a long ponytail hanging over his shoulder. The stranger had a belt around his waist with lots of tools dangling down his legs. He scared me with his gruff, booming voice. I thought he wanted to hurt me with one of those scary-looking tools. I started to bark and race around the yard in fear.

Poppa called to me, saying everything was okay, but I was too scared to listen to him. I picked up speed and raced past the stranger, through the open gate.

I ran around the front yard, not sure what to do or where to go. Poppa and the stranger ran after me, yelling at me to come back. The stranger jumped into his truck. It made a loud, roaring noise as he drove down the lane. He kept yelling at me to stop, but I was too scared to listen to him or Poppa. Maybe they wanted to hurt me. Maybe they thought I was bad puppy. I needed to keep running. I saw the front pasture and started racing down the gravel driveway. Australian shepherds can pick up a lot of speed with our powerful back legs. I ran as if my life depended on it. I was scared! I ran into the grassy pasture as the stranger drove his truck down the driveway, trying to get to the front gate before I did. Poppa was running after me as fast as he could run. I started to run even faster. My back legs pushed me forward like a jackrabbit; I used my front legs to leap ahead, covering as much ground as possible.

I raced to the front gate, but it was closed. I knew I could leap through the railings and be free. But where would I go? I had never been out there before. At the last second, I changed course, turning to the right and racing along the fence line. I could hear Poppa calling to me. *He must think I am a bad puppy*, I thought. *He is yelling. The stranger is yelling, too.* I need to keep running! I turned right again and headed up the grassy pasture, racing back toward the house. I know I felt safe when I was in the house. I forgot that it was Poppa who was chasing after me. All I could think was that if I got to the house, Momma and Poppa would be there, waiting for me. Maybe they would keep these men from yelling at me and chasing me.

I ran to the house, but I didn't know how to get inside. I could hear the men still yelling at me. Their voices were getting louder. I didn't know what to do. The gate to the backyard was closed. I raced around the garage in a panic.

The backyard fence was too high to leap over
without hurting myself. Just when I thought I'd have
to run back down the driveway and get away, I
spotted the back gate. It was a long metal gate that
was several feet lower than the wooden fence. I spun
around in two circles, picking up speed. Cody, Ace,
and Durango, the three horses that also live on our
ranch, saw me and ran over to the back pasture fence

to watch what I was doing. I raced toward the metal gate and leaped into the air with all the power I could muster. As I sailed through the air toward the backyard, I could see the house come into view on the other side of the shed. This was my home! Surely my Momma and Poppa would be there and would save me from the men.

I ran around the backyard, looking into the large back windows and hoping that Momma and Poppa would see me. Suddenly, the front gate opened and one of the men ran into the backyard. *What am I going to do?* I asked myself. I was going to have to leap over the metal gate again and run away. Just as I began to run in circles and pick up the speed needed to leap over the back gate again, I heard my Poppa's voice. *Adam! Thank God you are safe!*

I stopped racing around and looked at him. I was so glad to see my Poppa! He ran over to me, threw his arms around me, and hugged me tightly. I was safe!

Poppa took me inside the house. The stranger stayed outside and finished his work. I lay down, exhausted, and fell asleep in my crate. When I woke up, my momma was home. She and Poppa gave me rubs and told me how happy they were to have me home and safe. I was so relieved to know that they cared so much about me. That night, I went to sleep and dreamed about all the fun things I would do on the ranch with Momma, Poppa, and my friend the cat.

# *Chapter 4*
## Adam Destroys Mr. Ginger Man

I love to chew on things. It makes my teeth feel good. When I got to my new home, Momma had a nice toy waiting for me in my crate. It looked like a red ginger man cookie with big eyes sewn onto its round face. It squeaked when I picked it up.

Momma laughed each time I made the toy squeak, because I would tilt my head and perk my ears. I wondered why it made a noise each time I bit it.

When I curled up in my crate at night, Momma let me have my toy next to me. One morning, she came into the room and found me surrounded by white stuffing. I had fun during the night pulling the fluffy cotton out of my toy.

I found the little plastic bubble that made the toy squeak. Once I had accomplished that, I fell asleep. In the morning, I looked up just when Momma saw me laying there, surrounded by all the stuffing. *Oh no*, I thought, *she is going to yell at me for making a mess.* I jumped up and started using my nose to move the stuffing into a corner. I needed to clean up my crate for Momma. Instead of yelling at me, Momma just laughed. She opened the crate door, picked up the toy and stuffing, and put it all back together. She sewed it up again, squeaker and all! I was more careful the next time I played with my ginger man toy. Each night, I would rest my head on my toy and fall asleep.

One day, Momma took me to someone called a *groomer*. The woman bathed and brushed me and trimmed my fur. I don't really like to go to the groomer, but she does make me look very nice.

Momma left my ginger man toy with me so that I would have something familiar while I waited for her to pick me up.

When Momma returned, the groomer put a leash on me and walked me out to show Momma how nice I looked. I danced around and jumped up to kiss Momma for coming back to get me.

The groomer showed Momma what was left of my toy. While Momma was gone, I chewed and chewed on the ginger man. There was nothing left but scraps. I sat down and looked at the floor. Surely Momma would yell at me now. But she just laughed and told the groomer to throw away the scraps. She said I needed a *big boy toy*. Then Momma took me to the pet store and let me pick out a chew toy. It was a braided rope that was designed for puppies like me. It would make my teeth stronger, and it tasted like peppermint. I liked it! Momma let me hold it during the car ride home. I lay down in the back seat and held the braided rope in my paws. As Momma drove, my eyes began to droop. I couldn't stay awake. I dreamed of lying in my crate, tossing my new toy in the air, and listening to Momma laugh as she watched me play.

After that, my momma always had good puppy toys for me to play with and chew. She and Poppa understood that puppies need a good chew toy. I am such a lucky puppy!

# *Chapter 5*
## Adam Eats a Table

I try to always be a good puppy, but sometimes I get carried away. One morning, my momma and poppa were out for a run on the country road. They didn't take me running on the road because I was scared of the big trucks that sometimes roar down the road. While they were running, I ran around the house, playing tag with Tinker Bell, my cat friend. She is called Tinker Bell because she has a bell that hangs on her collar. Her little bell rings *ting-a-ling-a-ling* every time the cat runs across the room.  That makes it easy for me to find her if she tries to hide from me.

I chased Tinker Bell into the living room and around the couch. She ducked under the coffee table and stayed back just far enough that I couldn't reach her. I sat down and started to think about how I could get her. I still wanted to play, even if she didn't. I put my nose on the edge of the table so that I could rest while I thought about what to do.

Every once in a while, I would look down to see if my friend had crawled out from under the table. She hadn't. As I thought about what to do, I started to chew on the wooden edge of the table. The wood tasted like the sticks that Momma tossed to me when we were outside. It felt good on my teeth, so I kept chewing on the corner. I don't know how long I did that, but pretty soon my friend the cat ran past me, racing into the kitchen. I chased her and had her pinned, with my nose on her belly, when Momma and Poppa came home.

Momma stopped me from giving Tinker Bell any more pink-belly pokes. Momma was just about to take me outside to the backyard when Poppa saw what I had done to the living room table. He took me by the collar and made me look at the damage I had done to the table. I was so scared. I thought about how my first owner had yelled at me for chewing on furniture and how she left me at the pound as my punishment.

To make matters worse, I peed on the floor because I was so scared. I thought for sure Poppa would make me go back to the pound. I wanted to stay. I was so sorry! I couldn't even look at Momma. I was so ashamed.

Poppa put me in my crate while he and Momma cleaned up my messes. I put my head down and covered my nose with my paws. After I had stayed in my crate for a while, Momma let me go outside with her. I wanted to tell her that I was afraid to go outside. I thought she would put me in the car and take me to the pound. I put my nose in her hand to tell her I was sorry. She gave me a pat on my head and took me with her to the barn to see the horses. She told me she loved me but didn't want me to chew on anything but my toys.

That evening, Poppa gave me a pat on my head when he put me to bed in my crate. Maybe I was going to be able to stay here after all! I promised to be a good boy and not chew on the table ever again.

# *Chapter 6*
## Adam Gets a Wading Pool

I like to ride in the backseat of Poppa's big, blue pickup truck. He and Momma take me with them when we go to the pet store, because I can walk inside with them and not get in trouble. One hot summer day, we drove into town because Momma and Poppa wanted to get a wading pool for me. They said it would help keep me cool in the Texas heat, and I would have fun playing in the water. They were right!

When we got home, Poppa put my pool on the back patio and used a garden hose to fill it with cool water. I sat next to Poppa and turned my head from side to side, trying to figure out what was going on. Then Momma and Poppa took off their sandals and walked around in the pool, laughing as they splashed in the water. They called my name and asked me to jump in with them, but I was afraid. After a few minutes, I crept closer and put my nose over the hard plastic edge of the pool and stuck my tongue into the water to take a drink. I liked the feel of the cool water as it slid down my throat! Before I knew what was happening, I leaped into the pool and splashed around, too. It was fun because I could drink water while I walked around and kept cool.

After that, Momma would laugh every time I raced around the yard and took a flying leap into my pool.

One day, I kept leaping in and out of the pool. My wet paws got muddy when I raced around in the dirt of the back yard. Pretty soon, my pool went from clear, clean water to a brown, dirty mess. It made my white fur muddy.

Momma came outside and saw my mess, but she didn't yell at me. Instead, she pulled my pool out on the grass and dumped out the dirty water. Then she used the garden hose to clean all the mud from the bottom of my pool before filling it up again with clean water. I watched her as she walked inside the house and picked up some towels and a bottle of liquid. Before I knew what was happening, Momma had me in the pool and was giving me a bath. I don't like baths. Momma had to hold onto my collar to keep me from jumping out of the pool and running through the yard again. She rubbed my body and made me white with soapy suds. I decided that I do like that part of the bath. I just don't like it when Momma uses the garden hose to get me wet. The soap that Momma used is a special puppy product that smells like oatmeal. I like oatmeal! I like to lick my fur after Momma gives me a bath because it tastes good. Momma says I smell like a big oatmeal cookie! Momma used the garden hose to wash off all the soap. By that time, I'd had enough of the bath and was ready to jump out of the pool and shake off the water. When Momma finally let go of my collar and allowed me get out of the pool, I ran around the patio and tried to shake off the water. That made Momma laugh.

The best part of bath time is when Momma uses towels to dry me off. She holds a towel in her hands and stretches it as wide as she can. I leap in the air, and she grabs me and rubs me all over. It feels so good! Momma laughs when she wraps the towel around my body and watches me dance around the patio, peeking at her from under the towel as I squeal with happiness. Momma has to use two or three towels to get me dry. I get to roll around in each towel and enjoy all the attention that Momma gives me as she gets my fur fluffy again.

After my bath, Momma drags my wading pool back out to the grass and dumps out the water. Then she fills it up again so that the next time I'm out in the heat, I can jump into my wading pool and keep cool while I get a drink of water. I have a lot of fun in my wading pool!

# *Chapter 7*
## Adam and His "Nubbin" Learn to Run

Most Australian shepherds do not have a tail. Mine is just a stubby little bobtail, which is natural for my breed. Without a tail, I can tuck my hind end between my back legs and quickly spin out of the way of danger when I herd large animals. If I had a tail, it might get in the way as I tuck and spin my body. Or another animal could bite my tail and hurt me. Instead, I can easily get out of the way and run in a circle to keep control of an animal that weighs hundreds of pounds compared to my forty pounds.

My bobtail is very noticeable after my Momma takes me to the groomer and I get a short haircut, which is good for keeping me cool when I am running. Momma and Poppa tease me about my little bobtail. They call it a *nubbin*. When we are running, Poppa comes up behind me and lightly squeezes my little bobtail. He and Momma laugh as I leap into the air and give them wet kisses. It doesn't hurt me when they do that because I know they love me. It makes me want to jump into the air and race ahead on the trail as they chase me. Momma and Poppa can run fast for humans, but they can't keep up with me!

Aussie's have a lot of energy. We like to run, but Momma taught me to be a long-distance runner. One day she put me on the leash and started running down the long driveway. I ran with her. When I would try to run faster than she did, Momma would lightly pull on the leash so that I would slow down and run beside her. After a short time, I realized that Momma wanted me to run either beside her or just behind her. We had fun as I learned how to be a runner.

After about three weeks of learning to run up and down the driveway, Momma and Poppa took me to the nearby state park to run on trails. We would run for ten minutes and then walk for ten minutes.

Momma and Poppa wanted me to go slow and gain strength without hurting my paws. Many weeks later, I could run four miles without stopping. Momma taught me how to drink from a water bottle as we ran. She said that makes me a special puppy.

Now I can run the full loop of the trail. It is called Wolf Mountain loop and is eight miles long. When we are running on the trails at the park, a lot of people comment on how fast we can run around Wolf Mountain. Once we start running, there is no stopping us. It is a lot of fun! Momma tells people that she has *puppy power*—that's me! On the backside of the Wolf Mountain loop, the trail becomes difficult as it winds through the trees and becomes a steep climb up a rock-covered hill. Momma said I get an extra burst of puppy power as I leap up the rocks with her. Sometimes she leads me and sometimes I bound ahead and lead her.

When I run in front of Momma, she bends down and gives me a little squeeze on my nubbin. That makes me leap in the air and give her a wet kiss. We have fun when we go running, especially when we pass

other people and show them how strong we are!
Momma tells me that I am a lean, mean, running
machine. But I am not really mean, unless I think
someone is trying to hurt my momma. If that
happens, I pretend to be a fierce puppy. I bark at
people and stand in front of Momma to protect her.

Living with Momma and Poppa is wonderful,
especially since I get to run at the park and around
our ranch. I have fun running through the pastures.
There are lots of places to explore as I patrol the
property and keep everyone safe. When Momma
and Poppa are busy taking care of the horses in the
morning, I run out to the pasture and sniff around
the trees and grassy areas. I can smell the scent of
deer, rabbits, coyotes, and other animals that
wandered through the pasture the night before.

Once I saw a big buck in our front pasture. At first
I thought it was one of the horses. I ran down the
driveway to try and herd the horse back into the small
pasture. That's when I realized it was a male deer.
The big buck lowered its head when I ran toward it.

I could see the antlers on its head. I decided to run after him and chase him out of the front pasture. I wanted to tell him that the grass was for our horses, but he didn't stand still to listen to me. I chased him across the open field and watched him leap gracefully over the fence. Each time I am out in the front pasture, I look for the big buck. I think that I can run fast, but he is like a bolt of lightning racing across sky. Some day I hope I can run as fast as that buck!

One day I was running at home instead of at the park. Momma ran with me up and down our gravel driveway. When we run at home, Momma lets me run free instead of being on a leash. As we ran past the big tree that grows in the pasture near the driveway, I could smell the scent of the giant jackrabbit that lives in our front pasture. I ran into the pasture and jumped through the tall grass, toward the big tree. The scent of the jackrabbit became stronger and stronger. I ran around the tree, poking my nose in the grass, while Momma continued to run down the driveway. Finally, I found the big jackrabbit. He was hiding in the tall grass.

But when I poked my nose on his back, the jackrabbit jumped up from his hiding spot and ran across the pasture.

I took a quick look back to see where Momma was, and then I ran after the jackrabbit and nipped at his hind feet. I wanted to catch the jackrabbit to tell him how much fun I was having chasing him across the grass-filled pasture. But the jackrabbit didn't want to have anything to do with me. He kept leaping through the grass and jumped over the neighbor's fence to get away from me. I wanted to tell him that I wouldn't hurt him if I caught him, but I didn't get the chance.

I came so close to stopping the jackrabbit from leaping over the fence. I stood and watched him jump away from me, and then I turned and saw my Momma running back up the driveway. I raced through the grass with my white head bobbing up and down in the green pasture.

As I raced through the grass, I could also smell the scents left behind by Cody, Ace, and Durango. They leave their scent when they roll in the grass and dirt. Momma said that horses roll on the ground to scratch an itch or stretch their bodies. I do the same thing, but I don't make as much noise as they do. The horses like to roll around and then jump up off the ground and shake themselves off while they whinny and snort with happiness.

Sometimes I am having so much fun exploring in the pasture that I don't hear my Momma or Poppa calling me. When I do hear them, I run back to the barn to see if they are ready to play with me. Sometimes they have two of the horses saddled up and ready ride. I like to run through the pasture as Momma and Poppa ride the horses. When we are in the front pasture, I have fun running through the grove of trees, following the horses as they walk or trot around our property. I get to sniff all the animal scents while I run along with the horses.

One time, when I got too close to Momma and Durango, the horse put its head down to sniff my nubbin. With my Australian shepherd instinct, I spun around to keep the horse from biting my bobtail. I raced around the horse in a circle, barking to let Durango know I was the shepherd and was in charge of the trail ride. Momma and Poppa laughed and said I was a good puppy. What a great life I have on the ranch!

# *Chapter 8*
## Adam Makes New Friends

I like to play with the neighbor's dog. His name is
Jake. He is a lot bigger than me. Momma said Jake
looks like the cartoon dog, *Marmaduke*. He is an
orange-brown color, with a large head and big feet.
Jake is my best friend. He doesn't mind if I jump on
him and bark at him. He doesn't care if I race
around and try to herd him as if he was a young calf.
Jake and I have fun running and tumbling around in
the pasture. Momma watches us and laughs as we
play. When Jake has enough playing, he walks away
from me and wanders over to the horse tank to get a
drink of water.

I am too short to get a drink from the horse tank, so
Momma puts out a bucket of water that I can use as

my water tank. She calls it my *big boy bucket*. She laughs when she sees me drink from the bucket, because I keep my nose in the bucket but my eyes on Jake. I need to be ready to run, because he might sneak up on me when I am getting a drink.

Sometimes Rusty, another neighbor dog, comes over to play. Rusty is part Irish setter and part golden retriever. He is the color of a pumpkin and has a long, fluffy tail. Rusty likes to roll on grass and play with Jake and me. Rusty can move faster than Jake, but I am still able to catch Rusty and pin him to the ground. I stand over him until Rusty wiggles away.

Rusty is good around the horses. He helps his owner take care of ten horses. One day, Rusty came over when the ferrier was working on Ace and Durango's hooves. The ferrier trims the horses' hooves and puts new horseshoes on their feet. Rusty showed Jake and me how to lie down on the ground and catch the trimmings of the hooves in our mouths. Horse hooves are tasty treats for dogs. I like to catch a piece in my mouth and then run to the side of the barn and bury it like a bone. I have to be careful not to let Jake or Rusty see where I bury my treasure!

Once in a while, Chip, one of Rusty's friends, sneaks onto the ranch. Chip is a wiry Jack Russell terrier, who yips and yaps and bounces around the yard. I chase Chip away from the house when he gets too noisy. One time, I chased him across the front yard and almost nipped his curly tail. But Chip had a head start and just made it through the wire mesh fence before I got him. After that, Chip stayed on the other side of the fence and just watched me play with Rusty or Jake in the front yard.

I can play with Jake for hours and hours. It is so much fun. Sometimes it seems like play. Sometimes it seems like work because my Australian shepherd instincts come out and I try to herd Jake around the yard. He plays along with me for a while, and then he lies down on the grass and tells me he's had enough. When this happens, I proudly stand over Jake and protect him while he gets some rest. That is how I would treat an injured or baby animal if I was out in the field as a herd dog.

When I am in the house, I protect my friend Tinker Bell by standing over her. Just as if she were a baby lamb, Tinker Bell sits or walks beneath me. I walk slowly and use my nose to keep her just below my belly, because that is the best way for me to protect her. Sometimes she gets upset because I won't let her get away. She doesn't understand that I am just trying to protect her. I chase after Tinker Bell to get her back in place, but she hides under a table, just out of my reach. I lie down on the floor and watch her to make sure nothing happens to my little friend.

When she thinks I am asleep or not looking, she runs to another room. I like to chase her. We have fun playing tag. Sometimes I pin Tinker Bell on her back and poke her belly with my nose. Momma tells me to stop if I am getting too rough with Tinker Bell. I forget that she can't play as rough as Jake.

Tinker Bell will usually fight back when I get too rough. Other times, she ignores my roughness and just starts licking my face. That feels really nice. I lie down and let her lick my entire face. It tickles when she licks and cleans my ears. It makes me feel sleepy. If I move my head, Tinker Bell uses her paws to pull me back so that she can finish giving me a bath. When Tinker Bell thinks I am clean enough, we curl up together in my crate and fall asleep.

When I sleep, I like to roll over on my back with my legs in the air or propped up against the crate wall. When I do that, Tinker Bell has to get out of the way so that I don't roll on top of her.

Usually Tinker Bell goes into her kitty hut, a little dome of fabric and furry material that she likes to curl up against when she sleeps. Sometimes Tinker Bell jumps up on top of my crate and curls up on a towel that Momma keeps up there for her to lay on and stay close to me during the night.

I have so many good friends here on the ranch. We have a lot of fun!

# *Chapter 9*
## Adam Herds Goats

One day, I walked outside with Momma to help take care of the horses. Momma noticed that Cody, Ace, and Durango were all standing near the back gate, staring at something near the Spanish oak tree. I crawled under the fence and sat down next to Cody, the little Paint horse, who looks a lot like me. I tilted my head from side to side as I tried to see what Cody and the other two horses were looking at out there.

Momma walked through the gate and stood in the pasture, trying to see any movement in the tall grass. Suddenly, we all saw a baby goat leap into the air. After a few minutes, five or six other baby goats began to jump around in the tall grass.

I jumped to my feet. I had seen the bigger goats in the neighbor's pasture before but never on our property.

Momma looked at me and pointed to the goats. *Go get those baby goats, Adam! Send them home!* I had not had opportunity to herd goats before. But my instincts told me what to do. I raced into the pasture, making a wide circle so that the baby goats couldn't see me in the tall grass. Every once in a while, my little white head and copper-colored ears would pop up out of the grass as I looked carefully to see how close I was getting to the little goats. I circled around and ran up behind the baby goats. They were surprised to see me when I jumped out of the tall grass, just behind the herd of goats. They started to run. I ran in a small circle to keep them together as they moved toward the fence.

One by one, the baby goats slipped under the fence to the neighbor's pasture. The momma goats ran over to see why the babies were making so much noise. I stood at the fence and barked as if to say, *everyone is okay. Take care of your babies.*

I raced back to Momma. She was clapping her hands and shouting that I was a good boy. I raced around the horses and around Momma. Herding goats was a lot of fun!

The next night, Momma went out to check on the horses just before sunset. I was in the backyard, playing with Poppa, when I heard Momma call to me. *Come here, Adam! Come out and get the goats!*

Poppa opened the gate, and I raced out to the pasture. Momma pointed to the goats and told me to send them home. Poppa ran over to the fence to watch me in action.

There were seven goats this time. Six baby goats were standing together eating grass. The other goat looked much bigger and was by itself further down in the pasture. I circled around and herded the baby goats back toward the fence just as I had done the day before. After the last baby slid under the fence and ran to its momma, I turned and ran through the tall grass, toward the lone goat.

As I got closer, I could see that he was a very big goat. He must have been three times my size, but that didn't scare me.

I ran up behind the big goat and nipped at his heels, barking to tell him to go home. Instead of running toward the fence like the baby goats did, the big goat turned around and charged at me. This big goat was the Billy goat.

The Billy goat was the father of all those baby goats. He had horns and a long beard that hung from his chin. When he charged, I crouched down and stared him right in the eyes until he stopped in his tracks. He stared into my eyes. I didn't move. He didn't move.

After staring long and hard at the Billy goat, I
quickly decided that I needed to make myself look
as big and tough as I could. I leaped at Billy goat
and barked loudly to tell him I was the boss.

He jumped backwards and then turned and ran
toward the fence. I chased after him, nipping at his
heels to keep him moving. He almost got stuck as he
crawled back under the fence. But he squeezed
through and turned to look at me. I leaped into the
air and barked as if to say, and *you stay there or I'll
chase you again!* The Billy goat turned and ran
away.

I raced back toward Momma and Poppa. They were both very proud of me. I think I heard Poppa say that he might go buy some goats so that I could have a daily job of protecting and herding them on our property. That would be so much fun!

I have lived with my Momma and Poppa for almost a year. Now that I am getting older, Momma and Poppa said that I am ready to travel with them when they go on vacation. They bought a shiny, new horse trailer that has a camper attached in the front. The camper has a bathroom, a combined kitchen and living room area, and a bedroom. The trailer hooks onto my poppa's truck. All three horses will get to travel with us. Ace, Cody, and Durango will ride comfortably in the rear of the trailer. There is even room for a fourth horse, if we get another one. I get to ride in the truck with Momma and Poppa when we are driving, and stay in the living area with them when we camp. We are going to have many new adventures when we travel!

Living on the ranch is wonderful because I have so many things to do, a lot of friends to play with, and a good Momma and Poppa to take care of me. I forget that I ever lived any other place.

## *The End*

**www.austinaussierescue.org**

## A Message from Austin Aussie Rescue

The volunteers and foster caregivers of Austin Aussie Rescue are thrilled that Adam and his family have shared their story! Puppy Tales could be the story of many Australian shepherds who have the good luck to be rescued, and ultimately, find loving families who have been chosen to provide forever homes to these wonderful dogs.

There isn't anything much cuter than a fluffy Aussie puppy. Many people take them home without doing research ahead of time to learn about the needs and behavior traits of their new pet. After a few months, their cute fluff-ball is bigger, bouncier—and capable of making messes if not provided with proper training, socialization, and exercise.

Aussies are slow to mature. They don't generally grow out of puppy hood until they are two to three years of age. Many people can't wait that long for their dog to outgrow puppy behavior and calm down. As a result, many Aussies end up like Adam, left at a shelter. There are not enough resources and foster families to rescue them all, and some are not adoptable by the time they are abandoned. Fortunately, many are saved and are matched with people who are ready for the energy level and challenges a young Aussie offers.

We recognize many of the Australian shepherd actions and characteristics described in Adam's Puppy Tales. The Aussie is an active, intelligent, herding breed. Aussies generally love people. In addition to herding, they do well in any activity where they work closely with their human companions. They do not do well when left alone for extended periods, particularly if left in a back yard.

We know that readers will enjoy Adam's adventures and learn more about Australian shepherds. We hope that some readers will realize they could provide the right kind of home for an energetic, lovable dog, and will consider an Aussie adoption.

Austin Aussie Rescue is a foster care, home-based rescue organization concentrating on Australian shepherd dogs in the central Texas area. We operate entirely with volunteers, locating new homes for purebred Aussies that are taken to local shelters or, for whatever reason, cannot stay at their current home. We have found homes for more than 150 dogs since 2001. Since June 2004, Austin Aussie Rescue has been an affiliated chapter of the Texas Aussie Rescue Association, Inc. (TARA), a Dallas-based 501(c)3 charitable organization (see http://txaussies.com).

Austin Aussie Rescue maintains a page on Petfinder:

http://austinaussierescue.org.

To help us match people and dogs, an adoption application is available at http://txaussies.com/Adoption_Process.html.

For more information email us at austinaussierescue@hotmail.com.

Joann Starks, Coordinator
Austin Aussie Rescue
PO Box 10426
Austin TX 78766-1426

Cover design and book layout created by
graphic designers Rex Burns and Lori Owens
with JH&A Advertising of Austin, Texas.
JH&A provides proven solutions for advertising,
marketing communications and public relations.